KU-175-286

Sam

the wee fat dog

Ann McDonagh Bengtsson

Illustrated by Frank Rodgers

CORGI PUPS

To Johnny Bengtsson and John McDonagh

Series reading consultant: Prue Goodwin,
Reading and Language Information Centre,
University of Reading

SAM, THE WEE FAT DOG
A CORGI PUPS BOOK

First publication in Great Britain

PRINTING HISTORY
Corgi Pups edition published 1996
Reprinted in 1996, 1997 (twice)

ISBN 0 552 54942 8

Copyright © 1996 by Ann McDonagh Bengtsson
Illustration copyright © 1996 by Frank Rodgers

The right of Ann McDonagh Bengtsson to be identified as the
author of this work has been asserted in accordance with
the Copyright, Designs and Patents Act, 1988

Condition of Sale
This book is sold subject to the condition that it shall not, by way of trade
or otherwise, be lent, resold, hired out, or otherwise circulated without the
publisher's prior consent in any form of binding or cover other than that in
which it is published and without a similar condition including this
condition being imposed on the subsequent purchaser

Set in Bembo Infant

Corgi Pups Books are published by Transworld Publishers,
61-63 Uxbridge Road, Ealing, London W5 5SA,
a division of the Random House Group Ltd,
in Australia by Random House Australia (Pty) Ltd,
20 Alfred Street, Milsons Point, Sydney, NSW 2061, Australia
in New Zealand by Random House New Zealand Ltd,
18 Poland Road, Glenfield, Auckland 10, New Zealand
and in South Africa by Random House (Pty) Ltd,
Endulini, 5a Jubilee Road, Parktown 2193, South Africa

Printed and bound in Denmark by
Nørhaven Paperback, Viborg

Contents

Sam, the Wee Fat Dog's Rotten Picnic

Sam is a dog, a wee fat dog, who
likes to take life
very
very
easy.
He lives with Jim in a
bungalow on the edge of a little
town somewhere in Scotland.

Sam likes to spend most of the winter in front of Jim's fire, dreaming of sausages and juicy bones. With short legs and a fat tummy, he's just no good

out in the rain or snow. On bad,
squelchy days he goes... one two,
splosh, shiver... three four. Brr,
no fun at all!

In the summer, Sam loves to lie under the big tree in the garden, guarding his bone hole from the cat who lives next door with Mrs McGinty. Sometimes Jim takes Sam for a walk and that's just what happened one day last June.

When Jim got up, the sun
was shining fit to burst. "What a
lovely day," he thought. Then he
had a bright idea. "Why don't
we have a picnic? I'll go and
waken Sam."

Sam, the wee fat dog, was
still fast asleep in his basket,
snoring his head off, dreaming
about lots of sausages laid out
in a row. All he had to do was
walk along eating them. Then
he heard... "Sam, Sam, Sam..."

He nearly jumped through the roof. "Oh no, a sausage is talking back. Maybe I shouldn't have eaten so many." But it wasn't a talking sausage. It was Jim.

"Come on, you lazy dog. We're going on a picnic."

"What's a picnic?" thought Sam. "Is it like a bus? Where do you go on it?"

Jim was too busy to explain. He got two plastic bags and began to put in everything they both liked best.

He packed sandwiches,
cheesy crisps, an apple, a bar of
chocolate and a can of fizzy
orange for himself.

Sam sat drooling
and dribbling, his
tongue hanging out,
when he saw what
went into his bag.

"Oh, lovely... two sausages, doggy treats and a chocolate mouse. I'll just eat that stuff now, Jim." Sam pushed his nose into the bag.

"Oh, no you don't," cried
Jim. "That's the whole idea. We
take the grub with us and eat it
in a field."

"That's daft," thought Sam,
"but if it makes Jim happy, fine. I
don't care where we eat it, as
long as we eat it."

Jim put on his backpack. Off
they went, down the road, past
the post office, across the bridge
and up the hill. Sam's tummy got
emptier with every step and his
wee stubby legs grew more and
more tired by the minute.

"Jim, can't we stop soon?"
he panted.

Jim cut across the field.
"Nearly there, Sam. Isn't this
lovely?"

"Lovely, my foot," growled
Sam. "I want my grub..." Then
an awful thing happened.

Just as they got to the top of
the hill, puffing like engines, Sam
saw a big rabbit. Sam likes rabbits
because they look like cats with
long ears and they run away... but
they don't have nasty claws and
they don't spit.

"A rabbit!" yelped Sam. Off
he ran as fast as he could, his wee
legs going like mad and his
tummy wobbling from side to side.

"Come back, you daft dog," shouted Jim. "You're not to chase rabbits. They're too fast for you. Sam! Sam!"

Sam didn't hear a word. He ran right on. And as I'm sure you've guessed already, the rabbit dashed down a hole.

Sam tried to get after it, but
fat dogs don't fit in rabbit holes.
Poor Sam was stuck.

The rabbit ran out of another
hole and rolled about laughing.
Then the rest of his family came

out of twenty more holes in the hill
and they all rolled about laughing
and making fun of poor wee Sam.

Sam's bahooky was stuck up
in the air and his short back legs
waved about.

"Get me out! Oh, Jim, save me, it's dark in here. They'll come and bite my nose!" he yelped.

Jim came puffing up and started to pull Sam's legs.

"Oh, my legs, my legs," yowled Sam.

Jim got a grip round his
middle instead and gave a great
big tug. There was a... sssch...
schplopp, and Sam came flying
out on top of Jim... who fell
backwards right onto his
backpack.

Their lovely grub was
flattened and horrible. The
sausages and the chocolate mouse
got mixed up and the doggy treats
were smashed to smithereens.

Sam could have cried. "I'll eat it anyway, Jim," he whined. "It will taste the same. I don't mind."

"We can't eat that stuff, Sam," said Jim in disgust. "Och, this is a rotten picnic. Come on, we're going home."

The pair of them slunk
back, hungry and sad. Sam had
his tail between his legs and he
snuffled, "Whine and moan,
we're going home," all the way.

Just as they reached the gate,
feeling really sorry for themselves,

out came Mrs McGinty from next
door.

"What's the matter, you two?
Have you dropped a pound and
found five pence?"

"We've had a rotten picnic,
Mrs McGinty," explained Jim.

"And I've nothing left to eat in the house."

Poor Sam put his paws over his eyes and howled blue murder.

"Oh, you poor wee dog," said Mrs McGinty. "Listen, Jim, you cleaned the snow off the path for me last winter, and Sam fetches my paper in the mornings, even if he does chew it a bit as well. I've just made a load of pies and a big apple cake. Would you like some? I can give you a pint of milk, too, if you want."

"Oh, yes please! Thanks very much, Mrs McGinty." Jim was all smiles again.

Sam jumped up and licked any bit of her he could reach.

"You're a nice dog, Sam," she laughed, and went in to get the grub.

The sun was still shining, so
they sat under the big tree on a
rug from Jim's bed and ate the
pies and the apple cake. Then
they drank the milk.

"You know, Sam,
this is the best place
to have a picnic,"
said Jim.

"I could have told you that
if you'd asked me, Jim." Sam
wagged his tail and licked up the
last drops of milk.

Sam, the Wee Fat Dog
and the Holiday Hotel

Sam got up one Friday morning
and wandered over to his bowl.

"Oh, great, Popocops." He
licked the milk from his nose and
the last bit of cereal from the floor
where he'd dropped it. Then he
crawled back into his warm
basket for another little nap.

Jim came in and patted him on the head. "Sam! Sam! Don't go back to sleep. I've got to take you out to buy a few things before I leave you at the kennels."

That didn't mean anything to Sam at all, but he got up yawning and shaking himself anyway.

They bought some of Sam's
favourite food and stopped at the
butcher's for a bone. Sam was a
happy dog.

"Oh no, Sam,"
said Jim. "You're
not having the
bone now. It's for
when I leave you at
the kennels."

Sam whined a bit, but soon
forgot the bone since Jim was
doing strange things. He picked up
Sam's basket and his old chewed
slippers, then he put
them in the car.

"Come on, Sam, in you get,"
said Jim. Sam jumped in and sat
looking out of the window as Jim
drove off. After a bit, Jim stopped
at a big house.

Sam sniffed the air. "Dogs
and cats and chickens and pigs.
Where's this then?"

A little round lady with a big
wide smile came running out with
six dogs at her heels.

Sam was a bit scared. He put his tail between his wee fat legs and wished Jim would take him home.

"Don't you worry, Mr McKinley. Your wee dog will be just fine with us. I'll put him in the run next to Spotty. They'll be company for each other."

"I hope so, Mrs McWhirter, I've never left him before." Jim looked worried.

"Oh, he'll be grand," smiled the lady and led the way round the back to a row of big runs.

They were like long cages. Each
one had a little kennel at the end
and wire meshing between them.

Sam decided he didn't like
this at all. "I'm not going in
there." He dug in his back paws.

"Come on, Sam, it's just for two nights. I'll pick you up on Sunday morning," pleaded Jim, all red in the face as he tried to drag Sam inside the nearest run.

Finally Jim had to take out the bone and throw it right down to the end. "A bone!" Sam ran in and grabbed it. He was so busy chewing, he didn't even see Jim go.

After a while the bone
began to lose a bit of flavour, so
Sam looked around. Next door,
a big white dog covered in black
spots was lying fast asleep. It was
making little 'ooffl, ooffl' yelps,
and its paws twitched as if it was
running. Sam strolled over to the

wire mesh and woofed as loud as he could.

"Wha... wha..." The spotty dog jumped up and ran over, growling.

"Sorry I disturbed you," whined Sam, "but I don't know where this is."

"Oh, this is just the kennels," yelped his neighbour. "You know, a dog hotel. I come here for my holidays every year. It's very nice."

Sam wasn't sure about that. He just wished Jim would come and take him home. Head hanging, he crept back to his kennel and lay on Jim's old chewed slippers, feeling really

miserable. Sadly he thought
about the bungalow and his back
garden with the big tree and the
bone hole. "I'd even put up with
Mrs McGinty's cat if they'd let
me go home... nggnn... nggnn,"
he whined.

Later on, the lady came with
dinner for Spotty. He jumped up
and slobbered all over her.

Sam got a bit anxious.
"Maybe she won't give me any?
Maybe she doesn't know what I
like? Maybe I'll starve?" Poor
Sam. His ears drooped when he
saw her disappear again.

Then she came back with Sam's favourite food in his own bowl. She stayed and talked nicely to him while he ate.

"Never mind, wee fat Sam, we'll soon get a bit of that spare tyre off you. When you've finished eating, we're going for a walk."

"Walk?" Sam perked up right
away. He wagged his tail and
brought over his lead which Jim
had left in the basket.

"Oh, you're ready, are you?"
laughed the lady and clipped it
onto Sam's collar. "Come on,

then." She took three dogs on
their leads and a girl came too
with three more. You could hear
them in the next village, woofing
and yelping and having a great
time.

Sam's nose went mad with all
the new smells and his tail nearly
fell off his wee fat bahooky, it
wagged so much.

After a long walk, the girl gave each of them a bowl of water and some dog biscuits. Sam was so tired he didn't think twice about going into his run and he sank down in his basket for a quiet snooze.

When he woke up again, it
was dark. "W... ooff... www... oof!"
Sam wanted to sound brave but
he couldn't. Just then an owl flew
overhead and hooted...

Ooooo. It frightened the wits out
of Sam. He stuck his head into
his blanket, whining, "Blubber
and moan, I want to go home,"
and missing Jim like mad.

Spotty came up to the mesh.
"Hee, hee! Don't let it worry you,
Sam. The owl only eats mice.
You're too fat for him."

Sam didn't think that was
funny, but he felt a bit braver
anyway. "I wasn't scared," he
growled. "I was just looking for
my bone under the blanket."

Suddenly the dogs in the next
set of runs began to bark blue
murder. The whole place was one
horrible mangle of howls, woofs
and yelps. Sam was so frightened
he ran round in circles.

Mrs McWhirter came running out in her dressing-gown and slippers. "What's all this?" she shouted above the racket. "Oh my goodness, we've forgotten to lock the chickens in. Look, they're terrified! I think the fox has been here. I'd better lock them up."

After all the excitement, the dogs slept like bugs in a rug. Next day, out they went for lots of walks as usual. Sam woofed and sniffed so much, he wouldn't have heard an elephant let alone a fox that night.

Next morning, when he opened his eyes, he got a lovely surprise. Jim was holding the breakfast dish. It's hard to say who was the gladder – Jim or Sam – but they both looked fit to burst.

"Oh, I missed you, Sam," said Jim.

"Me too." Sam licked Jim all over his glasses, so he had to take them off to clean them.

"Thanks very much, Mrs McWhirter. Sam looks fine." Jim shook her hand.

"Oh, he was no bother at all, Mr McKinley... A wee bit scared to begin with, but he soon settled in."

"Scared? Me?" thought Sam. "Not a chance! I'd even have chased that fox if they'd have let me!"

Sam jumped into the car and lay with his head on Jim's knee all the way home, which made changing gear a bit difficult.

"Well, Sam, I think that was a good holiday hotel I found for you." Jim tickled his ears.

Sam looked up at him. "Hmmm... hotels are fine for a change, Jim," he thought happily, "but once in a while is enough."

THE END